A BOOK for BEAR

Written by
Ellen L. Ramsey

Illustrated by
MacKenzie Haley

FLAMINGO
BOOKS

Bear loved books.

Every day, Bear sat at the edge of
the woods and listened to a girl read.

The girl, whose name
was Ellen, loved to read.
Bear loved to listen.

Ellen read . . .

scary
books,

exciting
books,

funny
books.

Bear and Ellen loved them all.

One afternoon, sitting under their favorite tree,
Bear said, "I want a book of my very own. A book the
color of ripe red raspberries. And delicious to read.
Where do you find your books?"

"At school," said Ellen. "But bears aren't allowed. Tomorrow I'll bring you a new book."

"But," said Bear, "I want to pick it out for myself."
"Hmm," said Ellen. "Then we'll need a plan.
And I know just the thing."

The next morning, Ellen and a
furry superhero walked to school.

They tiptoed into the back of Ellen's classroom. "I've never seen so many books!" Bear whispered.

Bear rushed toward a bookshelf. He reached
for a book the color of ripe red raspberries,
but . . .

the teacher turned around. She pointed. She
screamed, "A bear! A bear! A bear at our school!"

Bear raced back to the woods with a cape, but no book.

After school, Ellen found Bear by their favorite
tree. "I'm sorry our plan didn't work," she said.

"But," said Bear, "I still want a book, and I want to pick it out for myself. Where else can I find a book?"

"The library," said Ellen.
"But bears aren't allowed."
"Don't worry," said Bear.
"I have a plan."

Ellen and a blueberry bush walked into the library.
"The library has even more books than your
classroom," Bear whispered. "Rows and rows of books!"

First the librarian saw
Ellen. Then the bush.
Then the bear.

The librarian shrieked, "A bear!
A bear! A bear in our library!"

Bear and Ellen raced back to the woods with blueberries, but no book.

"But," said Bear, "I still want a book, and I want to pick it out for myself. Where else can I find a book?"

"The bookstore," said Ellen. "But bears aren't allowed."
"Maybe I need a different disguise," said Bear.
"I know just the thing," said Ellen.

Ellen and a furry giant, wearing a coat and hat
and carrying an umbrella, tiptoed into the bookstore.
"So many, many books," Bear whispered. "There
must be a book for me."

Then Bear saw just what he wanted—
a book the color of ripe red raspberries.

He rushed for the book, but didn't see the ladder or the clerk on the ladder. Clerk, ladder, and furry giant, wearing a coat and hat and carrying an umbrella, crashed to the floor.

The clerk yelled, "A bear! A bear! A bear in our bookstore!"

Bear and Ellen raced back to the woods
with a broken umbrella, but no book.

"How will I ever find a book of my own?" asked Bear.
"Don't worry," said Ellen. "We'll think of something."

Bear scratched his back
on the tree and thought.

Ellen scratched the top of
her head and thought.

Suddenly Bear said, "Could we make a book?"
Ellen smiled. "Be right back."

She returned with paper and markers of every color, including, of course, raspberry red.

"What do you want your book to be about?" Ellen asked.

"I know just the thing." Bear whispered his idea to Ellen.

"A perfect plan," she said.

Ellen wrote and wrote.

Bear and Ellen drew picture after picture.
When they finished, Bear beamed.

"Will you read my book to me?"

"Of course," Ellen said.

Ellen opened the book and read,

"Bear loved books."

To my mother, Sarah Louise DeRolph Wampler, an artist and art teacher, who inspired in me my love of books, especially picture books!
—E. L. R.

For Megan, my favorite bibliophile.
—M. H.

FLAMINGO BOOKS
An imprint of Penguin Random House LLC, New York

First published in the United States of America by Flamingo Books,
an imprint of Penguin Random House LLC, 2023

Text copyright © 2023 by Ellen Ramsey
Illustrations copyright © 2023 by MacKenzie Haley

Library of Congress Cataloging-in-Publication Data is available.

Manufactured in China

ISBN 9780593527245

Special Markets ISBN 9780593692363 Not for resale

10 9 8 7 6 5 4 3 2 1

RRD

Book design by Lily K. Qian and Mackenzie Haley   Text set in Recoleta

This Imagination Library edition is published by Penguin Young Readers, a division of Penguin Random House LLC, exclusively for Dolly Parton's Imagination Library, a not-for-profit program designed to inspire a love of reading and learning, sponsored in part by The Dollywood Foundation. Penguin's trade editions of this work are available wherever books are sold.